It's time for
COWS IN ACTION!

Genius cow Professor McMoo and his
trusty sidekicks, Pat and Bo, are star
agents of the C.I.A. – short for
COWS IN ACTION!
They travel through time, fighting evil
bulls from the future and keeping
history on the right track . . .

Find out more at
www.cowsinaction.com

READ MORE STEVE COLE BOOKS!

C.I.A.

COWS IN ACTION

THE ROMAN MOO-STERY

Steve Cole

Illustrated by Woody Fox

RED FOX

THE ROMAN MOO-STERY
A RED FOX BOOK 978 1 862 30191 7

First published in Great Britain by Red Fox,
an imprint of Random House Children's Publishers UK
A Random House Group Company

This edition published 2007

5 7 9 10 8 6

Set in Bembo Schoolbook

Red Fox Books are published by Random House Children's Publishers UK,
61–63 Uxbridge Road, London W5 5SA

www.**randomhousechildrens**.co.uk
www.randomhouse.co.uk
Addresses for companies within
The Random House Group Limited can be found at:
www.randomhouse.co.uk/offices.htm

THE RANDOM HOUSE GROUP Limited Reg. No. 954009

A CIP catalogue record for this book is available from the British Library.

The Random House Group Limited supports The Forest Stewardship
Council® (FSC®), the leading international forest-certification organisation.
Our books carrying the FSC label are printed on FSC®-certified paper.
FSC is the only forest-certification scheme supported by the leading
environmental organisations, including Greenpeace. Our
paper procurement policy can be found at
www.randomhouse.co.uk/environment

MIX
Paper from
responsible sources
FSC
www.fsc.org   FSC® C016897

Printed and bound in Great Britain by Clays Ltd, St Ives plc

*For the dynamic dinolings of 3GR as was —
Morgan, Nadia, Lukas, Joseph, Pablo, Tom,
Kit B, Garry, James, Eden, Fiona, Kaia,
Fergus, Ollie, Mairna, Jimmy, Luis, Titus,
Lea, Eve, Shadeh, Phoebe, Sunee, Joss,
Caitlin, Milan, Kit V, Laura Wa, Tyler,
Laura Wh, Imogen and Yusuf — and for their
hard-working and resourceful teacher,
Suzanne Green.*

★ THE C.I.A. FILES ★

Cows from the present —
Fighting in the past to protect the future . . .

In the year 2550, after thousands of years of being eaten and milked, cows finally live as equals with humans in their own country of Luckyburger. But a group of evil war-loving bulls — the Fed-up Bull Institute — is not satisfied.

Using time machines and deadly ter-moo-nator agents, the F.B.I. is trying to change Earth's history. These bulls plan to enslave all humans and put savage cows in charge of the planet. Their actions threaten to plunge all cowkind into cruel and cowardly chaos . . .

The C.I.A. was set up to stop them.

However, the best agents come not from 2550 — but from the past. From a time in the early 21st century, when the first clever cows began to appear. A time when a brainy bull named Angus McMoo invented the first time machine, little realizing he would soon become the F.B.I.'s number one enemy . . .

COWS OF COURAGE —
TOP SECRET FILES

PROFESSOR ANGUS MCMOO
Security rating: Bravo Moo Zero
Stand-out features: Large white squares on coat, outstanding horns
Character: Scatterbrained, inventive, plucky and keen
Likes: Hot tea, history books, gadgets
Hates: Injustice, suffering, poor-quality tea bags
Ambition: To invent the electric sundial

LITTLE BO VINE

Security rating: For your cow pies only

Stand-out features: Luminous udder (colour varies)

Character: Tough, cheeky, ready-for-anything rebel

Likes: Fashion, chewing gum, self-defence classes

Hates: Bessie Barmer: the farmer's wife

Ambition: To run her own martial arts club for farmyard animals

PAT VINE

Security rating: Licence to fill (stomach with grass)

Stand-out features: Zigzags on coat

Character: Brave, loyal and practical

Likes: Solving problems, anything Professor McMoo does

Hates: Flies not easily swished by his tail

Ambition: To find a five-leaf clover — and to survive his dangerous missions!

Prof. McMoo's
TIMELINE OF NOTABLE
HISTORICAL EVENTS

4.6 billion years BC
PLANET EARTH FORMS
(good job too)

13.7 billion years BC
BIG BANG - UNIVERSE BEGINS
(and first tea atoms created)

23 million years BC
FIRST COWS APPEAR
(23 million is my lucky number!)

1700 BC
SHEN NUNG MAKES FIRST CUP OF TEA
(what a hero!)

7000 BC
FIRST CATTLE KEPT ON FARMS
(Not a great year for cows)

1901 AD
QUEEN VICTORIA DIES
(she was not a-moo-sed)

2550 BC
GREAT PYRAMID BUILT AT GIZA
(by an Egyptian geezer)

**31 BC
ROMAN EMPIRE FOUNDED**

(Roam-Moo empire founded by a cow but no one remembers that)

**1509 AD
HENRY VIII COMES TO THE THRONE**

(and probably squashes it)

**1620 AD
ENGLISH PILGRIMS SETTLE IN AMERICA**

(bringing with them the first cows to moo in an American accent)

**1066 AD
BATTLE OF HASTINGS**

(but what about the Cattle of Hastings?)

**1939 AD
WORLD WAR TWO BEGINS**

(or World War Moo as it is known to cows)

**2007 AD
I INVENT A TIME MACHINE!!!**

**2500 AD
COW NATION OF LUCKYBURGER FOUNDED**

(HOORAY!)

**2550 AD
COWS IN ACTION RECRUIT PROFESSOR McMOO, PAT AND BO**

(and now the fun REALLY starts...)

(about time!)

**1903 AD
FIRST TEABAGS INVENTED**

THE ROMAN MOO-STERY

Chapter One

A MORNING OF EMERGENCIES

It was just another quiet Thursday
morning at Farmer Barmer's sleepy
organic farm. Chickens pecked the corn
. . . pigs rolled in mud . . . sheep grazed
in the meadow . . .

And with a massive moo of alarm, a
large red-and-white bull came crashing
out of his cow shed and fell to his knees!

The bull was no ordinary bull. For a
start, he was wearing glasses and
clutching a screwdriver in one hoof. His
name was McMoo – Professor Angus
McMoo – and he was a brilliant
inventor. The cow shed he lived in was
no ordinary cow shed, either. After
months spent raiding the bins of the

3

scientist next door for electronic bits and pieces, Professor McMoo had made it a very special cow shed indeed . . .

"Quick!" cried McMoo. "Pat, Little Bo, get out of that paddock and into the shed, now! It's an emergency!"

And with that, he charged back inside.

"An emergency?" Pat Vine, a young bull, turned to his older sister in alarm. "I wonder what's happened."

"Who cares, as long as it's exciting!" cried Little Bo happily. She ran for the gate that separated their paddock from the professor's yard. "I've been practising my boxing moves. I'm itching for the chance to give someone a hoof sandwich!"

Pat frowned as he charged after her. "You can't solve every problem just by whacking it, you know!"

"Can!"

"Can't!"

"Can!" They reached the gate, which was chained shut. Bo smashed it to bits with a karate cow kick and smiled triumphantly at Pat. "See?"

Pat sighed. Sometimes he found it hard to believe that he and Bo were related. While he was quiet and thoughtful and liked to puzzle stuff out, Bo was a wild, impulsive milk-cow who liked fighting and dying her udder strange colours (today it was aquamarine). But they were both clever cows, from the same breed as Professor McMoo. Scatty, fun and always energetic, the professor was their guardian, their guru and their best friend.

But why was he suddenly in such a flap?

"Pat! Bo!" he yelled again from the cow-shed doorway. "Come on, it's urgent!"

Pat and Bo rushed over.

"What's up, Professor?" Pat panted. "What's the emergency?"

"Can I whack anyone?" added Bo hopefully.

McMoo looked serious. "Come into the shed. I'll show you what's happened."

So Pat and Bo bustled inside. The wooden walls were stained and scuffed, hay littered the floor and cobwebs cloaked every corner. It looked so grotty, no one would ever have guessed the incredible truth . . .

"Brace yourself, you two." McMoo sighed. "I'm afraid—"

"What is the meaning of this?" came a dreadful screech from outside. "You stupid steak-brained vandals have gone too far!"

7

Pat gulped and peeped out through the doorway. A large, blubbery woman was jumping up and down with rage in front of the broken gate. She looked like a giant bullfrog trying to lay a square egg, only not quite as attractive.

"Now look what you've done, Bo!" he groaned. "Bessie Barmer's going round the bend!"

"Huh!" snorted Bo. "She went there a long time ago, if you ask me."

Bessie Barmer was the farmer's wife. She was an old ratbag who hated all animals and was always plotting to send them off to the butcher's. Which was why Professor McMoo had turned his extraordinary mind (and his lifelong love of science and history) to the challenge of turning his cow shed into a very special machine. A machine that would allow him and his friends to escape the farm and their fast-food fate . . .

A *time* machine!

But they hadn't counted on the arrival of mysterious cows from the future. Cows who persuaded McMoo, Pat and Bo to join the crime-busting, time-busting C.I.A. – short for Cows in Action. Now the three of them had a secret life, travelling through time on dangerous adventures . . .

But as far as Bessie Barmer was concerned, they were just silly cows.

"The ancient Romans had the right idea," Bessie growled. "Like my great ancestor, Bessium, who ran the Roman Games. She threw cattle into the arenas and made them fight wild animals till they were squished. What a laugh! I wish I'd been there . . ."

"I'll show her squishing!" cried Bo, getting up on her back legs and waving her front hooves, while Pat struggled to hold her back.

"No, Bo," said Professor McMoo. He kicked away a bale of hay to reveal a large bronze lever. "We haven't got time to waste on Bessie Barmer. Get those doors closed, quick!"

Bo did so, just as McMoo yanked on the lever, and a rattling, clanking noise started up. Panels in the walls swung round to reveal futuristic flashing controls. A large computer screen swung down from the rafters. A huge horseshoe-shaped bank of switches and buttons poked up from the muddy ground to fill the shed's centre, along with a large wardrobe stuffed full of clothes from all times and places. The cow shed was becoming a Time Shed, ready to travel to any place on Earth in the past or future.

"What was that noise?" Bessie Barmer's snarling voice carried to them from outside. "I know you're hiding in there! I'm gonna make mincemeat out of you!"

"Better get out of here," said McMoo, twisting and turning the Time Shed's controls. A hissing, swooshing sound started up. The ground lurched beneath their hooves, and bright purple light peeped in through cracks in the walls as the control centre shuddered and shook, faster and faster . . .

"We're off!" shouted McMoo.

Pat and Bo clung to one another as the Time Shed sped across the seas of time. "But where are we off to, Professor?" Bo demanded.

"To the year 2550," McMoo proclaimed. "To the Palace of Great Moos, in the land of Luckyburger."

"But . . ." Pat stared at him. "That's where the C.I.A. has their headquarters! Why are we going there?"

"Are all our friends OK?" asked Bo anxiously.

"We're going there because something truly terrible has happened," said McMoo. "Pat, Bo, I don't know how to tell you this . . ."

"Try quickly!" said Bo.

"Well," McMoo went on, "I was just about to check the hypertime transit systems, when I realized . . . we've run out of tea bags."

There was a long silence.

"Tea bags?" Bo echoed.

Pat frowned. "We're going all the way to the twenty-sixth century to pick up some tea bags?"

BUMP! The Time Shed landed.

"It's a serious matter!" McMoo protested. "Normally I'd ask Bo to raid Farmer Barmer's supply in the kitchen, but I heard him tell Bessie that he'd run out too. Besides" – he grinned at them

13

both and opened the doors – "it's been seven days since our last mission for the C.I.A. One whole week! I don't know about you lot, but I fancied a bit of excitement!"

"And you'll get it too," came a gruff voice. A hefty black bull with curly horns stood in the large marble hall outside. He wore a dark suit and shades, and a bright blue sash around his waist.

"Yak!" Bo ran out of the time machine, jumped into his arms and almost squashed him flat. "How's the Director of the C.I.A. this morning, then?"

"Worried," Yak admitted, quickly putting her down. "Hey, Professor. Hi, Pat. I was just about to send you an urgent message. We've got an emergency here."

McMoo stared in alarm. "Don't tell me you've run out of tea bags too?!"

With a sigh, Yak clicked his hoof.

Three cow maids quickly appeared with trays of steaming tea. Pat and Bo had a cup each, while McMoo was given a large plastic bucket. He drained it dry in moments. "Ahhhh, that's better." He smacked his lips. "Now, what's up?"

"I wish I knew," said Yak. He led the way across the marble floor into a super-cool meeting room. "All I do know is that the F.B.I. is up to something big this time . . ."

A prickle went down Pat's back. F.B.I. was short for Fed-up Bull Institute, the C.I.A.'s biggest enemies. They were always trying to muck up history and turn peaceful cows into savage, warlike creatures.

"Take a look at these pictures," Yak went on. He pressed a button and images appeared on the wall. They showed a huge, terrifying figure with glowing green eyes smashing his way through a shop window, robotic arms full of high-tech circuits.

"A ter-moo-nator," said McMoo grimly. "Half robot, half bull and all nasty. They're the F.B.I.'s deadliest agents."

Yak nodded. "Ter-moo-nators have been robbing electronics stores all over the country and taking the loot back in time . . ."

"Where are they taking this stuff?" asked Pat.

"*When* are they taking this stuff?" Bo added.

"That's just the problem – we don't know!" Yak sighed. "The F.B.I. has found a way to jam our time-trackers, so we can't tell where they're going."

Suddenly, the meeting room shook with a massive explosion!

"What was that?" gasped Pat.

Bo cheered. "Let's find out!"

Professor McMoo led the way out of the room alongside Yak. Cows were milling about in alarm. Huge chunks of marble lay scattered in the palace hallway. A big hole had been blasted in the floor.

And climbing out from inside the hole was a ter-moo-nator . . .

Chapter Two

CHASE THROUGH TIME

"A ter-moo-nator, here?" spluttered Yak.
"In the Palace of Great Moos?"

"Nowhere is safe from the F.B.I.,"
sneered the ter-moo-nator in a deep,
mechanical voice. "We can rob
anywhere!" As cow workers scattered in
panic, he climbed out of the hole with a
handful of electrical parts. Letters and
numbers on its steel chest revealed his
name to be T-117.

"Where did the ter-moo-nator get
those parts, Yak?" asked McMoo
urgently. "What's underneath us?"

"The private garage," Yak realized.
"All the very latest air-cars and

18

travel-pods are parked down there."

"C'mon, boys," yelled Bo. "Let's park T-117 down there too!" She started to charge towards the robo-bull – just as it pulled out a massive ray gun!

"Get down, Bo!" shouted Pat, rugby tackling her to the floor.

As the ter-moo-nator opened fire, Professor McMoo butted a slab of marble across the floor to block the path of the energy ray. The stone glowed white, then disappeared.

"That was a good tackle, Pat," said Bo approvingly. "And nice work from you too, Professor!"

Yak dragged them both clear as T-117 fired again. The death rays missed them all by centimetres. Then the robo-bull produced a large silver platter – an F.B.I. portable time machine – and jumped on top of it.

"Mission completed. Activating time jump." At once, T-117 started to disappear in a cloud of black smoke.

"He's getting away!" roared Yak. "And with our time-trackers jammed, we don't know where he'll end up."

"To the Time Shed, quick!" cried McMoo. "The ter-moo-nator doesn't have much of a head start. If we're fast, maybe we can follow his trail through time."

"You're brilliant, Professor!" said Pat happily, chasing after him into the Time Shed.

"See ya, Yak!" Bo blew him a kiss as she jumped inside too. "We'll stop that ter-moo-nator, just you wait!"

"Good luck!" Yak shouted.

Then the time shed glowed purple and disappeared.

Inside, Professor McMoo ran around the control room like a mad bull, flicking switches and pulling levers. The large screen hanging down from the rafters showed bright purple patterns.

Bo frowned. "Is the screen on the blink?"

"No," said the Professor. "That's what's outside – the passage of time. We're whizzing along it at eighty years per second, chasing after *that*."

Pat looked closely. He could see a

small, gleaming figure up ahead, riding a silver platter like a surfboard. "The ter-moo-nator!" he realized.

"He's going faster than we are!" Bo exclaimed. "He's getting away!"

"I'll try to boost our speed," called McMoo. "Watch the screen closely, Bo. The moment that ter-moo-nator disappears – moo at the top of your lungs. When she does, Pat, you must pull that yellow lever at once. Got it?"

"Got it," Pat and Bo chorused.

"Here goes, then!" McMoo twisted

five controls at once! Sparks exploded all over the Time Shed, and it shook and spun like a fairground ride. The over-stuffed wardrobe burst open and clothes flew about like crazy bats.

"Two hundred years per second," gasped the professor, blue sparks zapping all around him.

"We're catching up with the ter-moo-nator!" said Bo, hanging on to the screen. "Hang on, I think he's . . . MOOOOOOOOOOOOO!"

At her signal, Pat pulled the yellow

lever. It was like slamming on the brakes! With a squealing, scraping sound, the Time Shed stopped spinning and landed with a crash back on Earth.

"Phew," said McMoo, wading through piles of clothes to reach the destination meter. "Well, I'll be a calf's kipper! The ter-moo-nator has led us to ancient Rome in the year 64 AD. That's the year of the Great Fire of Rome!" He shook his head in wonder. "It went on for days and days. Two-thirds of the city burned to the ground."

"That's really interesting, Professor," said Bo, dropping down from the computer screen. "But I'm going after the ter-moo-nator – he's not getting away from ME!" And before McMoo and Pat could stop her, she had thrown open the doors and gone charging outside.

"Wait, Bo!" McMoo hollered after her, stuffing a silver ring through his nose and passing one to Pat. "You forgot your ringblender!"

Pat pushed his own ringblender into place. They were a brilliant C.I.A. invention. Cows who wore one could pass themselves off as human beings, blending in perfectly – just so long as they wore the right clothes. The special rings also translated any language. But only humans could be fooled by ringblenders. A cow would still recognize a ter-moo-nator – and a ter-moo-nator would recognize a cow . . .

"Professor, we've got to stop Bo!" said Pat, snatching up a white toga from the piles of clothes on the floor. "If the Romans see a mad cow running about, it might start a panic!"

"That's if T-117 doesn't zap Bo straight away," said McMoo, struggling into a blue toga. "Come on!"

The Time Shed had landed in a shady vegetable store. Pat and the professor

plunged outside into the clatter and
bustle of a busy Roman street.

They stared round in wonder. The sky
was blue over red-tiled rooftops and
white concrete temples and porches
propped up with pillars. The smell of
fresh herbs and the sound of chatter
filled the air. Men argued with traders
over the price of their goods.
Moneychangers jangled pouches of

coins to attract customers. Roman nobles swanned about, surrounded by bodyguards and eager tradesmen trying to sell them sandals and statues and potions and pearls.

But there was no sign of Little Bo or the ter-moo-nator.

McMoo and Pat forced their way through the crowds. No one looked at them twice – as far as the humans were concerned, here was just another Roman citizen with his son, out for a walk in the markets.

"Has anyone seen a cow?" McMoo yelled. "You can't miss her – she's got a greeny-blue udder and an attitude problem!"

A rich woman being carried on a couch by four slaves glared at him. "Yes, I've seen her. She was going faster than a chariot in the races – nearly knocked me flying!" The woman pointed down a side street. "She went that way!"

"Let's hope we catch up with her," said McMoo, "before she finds trouble... or trouble finds her!"

Unfortunately, Bo being Bo, she was already hot on the trail of big trouble.

She had bounded out of the Time Shed and charged down half a dozen streets in search of the ter-moo-nator. But he was nowhere to be seen.

"Oi! Toga-face!" she shouted, grabbing a passing businessman. "Have you seen an ugly robot bull anywhere?"

The man fled in fright, talking in a language she couldn't understand. Other people too were gawping and gaping all around her. "Oh no," she groaned, clutching her ringless nose. "I'm standing out like Bessie Barmer at a fashion show! I'd better get back to the Time Shed ..."

But as she stared around at the temples and courtyards and clean white villas, she realized she was lost!

"How totally annoying," grumbled Bo. Then she saw a sign with a picture of a bull drawn onto it, pointing down the street. Underneath the picture was written *Forum Boarium*. "Whatever that means," she said, sighing. "Still, anything to do with bulls has got to be worth chasing up . . ."

Ignoring all the funny looks she got, Bo followed the sign and kept trotting until she reached a long, low rectangular building lined with endless old pillars. There were fewer people around here – probably because there wasn't much to see. The building was obviously closed down, the entrance blocked up with wooden planks and more signs covered with funny writing.

"Forum *Bore*-ium, more like!" snorted Bo. "What a dump. They should paint it pink and kit it out with a killer sound system . . ."

Then suddenly, her ears pricked as she heard the sound of distant mooing. What were cows doing inside a closed-down building?

Maybe, just maybe, the ter-moo-nator was in there too . . .

"Geronimoooooooo!" yelled Bo as she ran up and took a flying leap over the barrier. She landed neatly on the other side – then hurtled away through winding passageways of stone, trying to find her way to whoever had made the moo.

Finally, she burst out into a large open courtyard, boxed in on all sides by two levels of seating. *Funny*, she thought, looking all around. *Looks a bit like an arena.* She could almost imagine Roman gladiators charging about, fighting each other for their lives . . .

Then, suddenly, three armoured figures came bounding into the arena.

Bo blinked. "Wow, I've got a good imagination!"

Then she blinked again, in disbelief. Because the three gladiators that stood before her were not Roman slaves or human fighters – they were bulls. Bulls wearing helmets and breastplates and carrying swords and nets and spiky shields …

They were very real. And they were rushing towards her, ready to attack!

Chapter Three

THE MOO-STERY DEEPENS

"So it's a fight you want, huh?" Bo cried as the three gladiator bulls closed in. One was tall, one was short, the other was skinny – but they all looked mean. "Well, step up, boys – and eat my hooves!"

The skinny one tried to throw his weighted net over her. But Bo dodged out of the way just in time and shoulder-charged the short one with the spiky shield. With a moo of pain he crashed to the ground.

The third gladiator lunged forward and swiped at Bo with his sword. "I saw that coming a mile off, tall-boy," she snarled, squirting him in the eyes with milk from her udder. "But you can't see at all" –  as he fell back spluttering, she whacked him on the nose with a double-hoofed haymaker – "can you?"

Suddenly a net was thrown over her head – the skinny bull had crept up behind her. She kicked out with her back legs and sent him flying. But no sooner had she wriggled out of the trap than his friend with the shield was coming at her again.

"I was saving these boxing moves for Bessie Barmer," she said, clobbering him. "But I guess they'll do for you too!"

The bull with the shield collapsed in a heap of hooves – but by now the other two gladiators were ready to attack once more.

Bo karate-chopped one and tail-whipped the other. They fell to their knees, and Bo sat down, panting for breath.

Then she heard hoofsteps behind her. Turning, she found two more gladiator bulls running towards her!

"This isn't fair!" she cried. The two new gladiators loomed over her . . .

But then, to her amazement, they held out their hooves to help her up!

Behind them, a large white water buffalo with enormous handlebar horns was striding over from the seating area with a gladiator's helmet. He placed it on her head.

"This helmet contains a special translator," he said. "My name is Lanista. Can you understand me?"

"Yes." Bo frowned and nodded.

"Good little Roman cow," said Lanista with a nasty smile.

He thinks I'm a local from this time,

34

Bo realized, and decided it was safer to
let him go on thinking that.

"What is your name?" he asked.

Bo struggled to think of a make-
believe name she could give him.
"Umm . . ."

"Umm, eh? Funny name." Lanista
frowned. "Funny-coloured udder too."

"Err . . ." Bo thought fast – but not

very convincingly. "It's . . . a birthmark."

"Hmm," said Lanista. "Well, young Umm with the unusual birthmark, you have passed the first stage. Now you may rest before beginning stage two."

"Stuff your stage two!" Bo replied. "What is this place? What are you on about?"

"Poor, simple cow!" cried Lanista. "The Forum Boarium is a cattle market, where the likes of you were bought and sold by humans before Emperor Nero closed it down. And the Fed-up Bull Institute has a better use for it now . . ." He chuckled, then looked at the three fallen gladiators and clapped his hooves. "Take these fumbling fools to pay the price of their failure. But first, take the girl to the pens to recover."

The two new gladiators nodded. As they dragged Bo away, she didn't struggle. She knew she had pitched up in the middle of a mysterious F.B.I. plot.

She had to stay here and find out all she could.

She only hoped that Pat and the professor would be all right without her . . .

Professor McMoo and Pat had not found Bo or the ter-moo-nator. But they had found a famous landmark, and McMoo was now very excited.

"The Circus Maximus!" he cried, staring up at the line of stone archways that seemed to stretch on for ever. "The first and largest Circus in Rome, as long as five football pitches laid end to end and with space for 250,000 people inside – imagine that! I've seen pictures of it in history books, but now we're seeing it for real. Imagine *that*!"

"Yep, it's amazing, Professor," said Pat kindly. Sometimes, McMoo's pleasure at parading through the past took his mind off a mission. So while the professor burbled on merrily, Pat was looking around the busy street for any clues that might help them in their search.

"Circus Maximus means 'Greatest Circus' in the Romans' language, Latin, but the things that happened here weren't very great, oh no." McMoo went on, "Chariot races, mainly. Twelve chariots racing around and around for four miles! You can imagine the accidents. Dreadful accidents!"

"Wonderful accidents, you mean!" came a sour woman's voice beside them. "A good crash always gets more people buying tickets – and as chief ticket seller, that means more cash for me!"

Pat gulped. "I recognize that voice...." He whirled round to find a familiar, ugly, red face on a familiar, fat, bullfrog body. There, sitting beneath the nearest arch, was the double of their enemy from the farm, Bessie Barmer!

"Oh no," groaned McMoo. "Not

another of Bessie's ancestors. We seem to meet one wherever we go!"

"And they're always horrible," Pat added.

"What are you two moaning on about?" the woman said. "It's me who should be moaning. Me, Bessium Barmus. I mean, since Emperor Nero cancelled all the races and closed down the Circus, I can't earn a crumb!"

"The Emperor Nero!" McMoo beamed. "He's famous for fiddling while Rome burned."

"He's fiddling me out of stacks of cash!" Bessium grumbled.

"But why has he closed the Circus?" McMoo asked her.

"He's closed the cattle market too – for redecorating, he says." She sighed.

"What's he going to shut next, eh?"

Pat hoped Bessium's mouth was on the emperor's list.

"Funny, though," said McMoo. "I thought Nero loved chariot racing."

"He does," Bessium snapped. "He's promised the people that bigger, better, badder chariot races are on the way. Races the likes of which the world has never seen . . ." She snorted. "Fine talk – but talk doesn't put bread on my table. And I can't even get a decent night's sleep these days, thanks to the ghosts."

McMoo frowned. "What ghosts?"

"I hear them all through the night, inside the Circus," she said. "They growl like angry giants! Roar like demented demons!"

Pat looked nervously at McMoo. "I don't like the sound of them." He lowered his voice. "Do you think T-117 could have anything to do with this?"

"He could," McMoo murmured.

41

"I'd like to hear these ghosts for myself. It seems we've got quite a Roman mystery on our hands." He chuckled. "Or do I mean moo-stery?"

But even as he spoke, a scary, rumbling, roaring noise started up – not from the Circus, but from the ground beneath them. People started to run about and shout in alarm.

"The ghosts!" squawked Bessium, wobbling like a giant jelly. "The ghosts are here in broad daylight! EEEK!"

"Something's here all right!" shouted

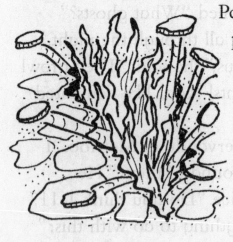 Pat as the paved street split open down the middle – and flames and smoke belched out from inside ...

Chapter Four

FIRE, FLOOD AND MARROWS

The Roman street erupted in chaos.
Slaves and citizens ran screaming in all
directions, blinded by the choking
smoke.

"Help! Help!" shouted Bessium
Barmus. "We're dooooooomed!"

Choking on the black fumes, Professor
McMoo hooked his horns around Pat's
neck and tugged him into the safety of
an archway as the flames leaped higher
from the crack in the road.

"Thanks, Professor," gasped Pat. "I was
very nearly a flame-grilled burger
there!"

"Shh," said McMoo. "Listen. That

43

roaring noise has stopped. Bessium's ghosts seem to have gone."

"But the fire's still here!" Pat shouted as bright orange flames crackled out of the split. "What's happening — is this the start of the Great Fire of Rome?"

"I don't think so. That started above ground." McMoo sniffed and frowned. "And that smells like oil to me . . ." He burst out coughing. "Stupid smoke, it's making my eyes water."

"Water!" gasped Pat. "Quick, Professor, there's a fountain further up the street. We could get some buckets and use the water to put out the flames."

"Never mind the buckets!" said McMoo, peering at the fountain through the smoke. "Judging by the thickness of that stone, if I charge into it at twenty-seven miles an hour from this angle, and you bash into the other side at about nineteen-and-a-half miles an hour—"

"Let's do it!" cried Pat. He didn't know what the professor's plan was, but he was determined not to let him down. Most of the crowds had fled by now, so he had a clear run at the fountain. Lowering his head he sprinted towards it. Through the thick smoke he glimpsed the professor thundering towards the fountain from the other side, and then—

WHAMMM! Pat and McMoo's hard heads and horns smashed the stone to pieces. Water came flooding out in a miniature tidal wave and sloshed down

the street. It poured into the crack in the street and put out the flames! Steam hissed out like someone had boiled a billion kettles under the ground.

Pat rubbed his dizzy head. "Your idea worked, Professor!"

"But what set off that earthquake and started the fire in the first place?" wondered McMoo, rubbing his tender horns. He walked over to the jagged split in the ground and peered down through the steam to see.

It was gloomy and dark down there, but he thought he could see the bronze gleam of a large, metallic object. Then, right beside it, two small green lights snapped on in the smoky shadows like eyes staring up at him.

The eyes of a ter-moo-nator!

"Pat, come here, quickly!" said McMoo. "I think I saw our old friend T-117!" But by the time Pat had got there, the green lights had gone.

And above ground, with a fanfare of trumpets, somebody else had arrived.

"Be silent, all, and lend your ears!" boomed a deep voice. "The glorious Emperor Nero wishes to speak to you!"

McMoo jumped up in amazement. A chubby man with curly hair had appeared in the street, surrounded by a gaggle of dignified old men. He wore a white toga trimmed with gold and a crown of laurels on his head. The people who had fled the street came rushing back to see their emperor, in awestruck silence.

"It's Nero!" McMoo was almost jumping up and down on the spot in excitement. "Look, Pat. A real, live Roman emperor right in front of us!"

"Shhh!" hissed a woman nearby as Nero cleared his throat to speak.

"Friends, Romans, and the rest of you," he began, looking a little flustered. "Do not be afraid, I can explain all that

 has happened here." He smiled. "As you know, I have closed the Circus Maximus while I make certain ... improvements. One such improvement will be heated seating, so your bottoms don't freeze on those chilly winter nights."

"Ahh, that's thoughtful," someone said fondly.

"Sadly, as you saw, my underground heating pipes have just exploded, so you'll have to freeze your bums off as usual," Nero went on.

Bessium Barmus peered out from behind a pillar, wiping soot from her face. "When will the Circus open again?" she demanded.

"Soon," Nero promised. "Very soon.

But in the meantime, to cheer everyone up, I shall hold a special event at the Circus this very night!"

"YES!" bellowed Bessium. She did a victory dance that threatened to set the whole street shaking.

"What about the ghosts?" someone shouted.

"There are no such things as ghosts," said Nero crossly.

"Maybe not," called McMoo. "But, even so, great Nero . . . is it wise to open the Circus tonight?"

"Shut up!" Bessium snarled. "He can open it if he wants to!"

McMoo ignored her. "I don't think underground heating pipes caused this destruction. Something else might be going on."

"Oh, really?" Nero looked at him crossly. "And who might you be, sir?"

Pat piped up. "This is the great Professor McMoo, who put out the fire!"

"With the help of young Pat here," McMoo added.

"McMoo, eh?" Suddenly, Nero smiled warmly. "It seems I have much to thank you for, my two friends. Perhaps you would care to join me at the palace for supper, as my guests?"

The crowd cast envious looks in McMoo and Pat's direction. McMoo bowed humbly. "It would be an honour," he said.

"Splendid!" Nero clapped his hands, and a bunch of slaves ran along the street with trowels and buckets full of thick white plaster. "My slaves will soon repair this little mishap in the road, and it will be as if nothing ever happened."

McMoo turned to Pat, his eyes boggling. "Supper with Emperor Nero – imagine that!"

"But did you imagine seeing that ter-moo-nator under the street?" said Pat grimly.

"I don't think so. And when we get to the palace, I must warn the emperor that all of Rome could be in great danger . . ." The professor nodded to himself. "Pat, you're faster than me – run back to the Time Shed, in case Little Bo is waiting for us there." He pressed Bo's ringblender into the young bull's hoof. "If she isn't, leave her this beside the door and write a note telling her to come to the emperor's palace straight away. Then, rush back and join us there yourself."

"Understood," said Pat, slipping the ringblender into his pocket. "I'll be with you as soon as I can!" And with a quick salute to Emperor Nero, Pat hurried away.

Pat was very good at finding things, and it didn't take him long to retrace his steps all the way back to the busy market street where the Time Shed had first arrived.

It was cool and quiet inside the
vegetable store, and Pat found it a
welcome change after running in the
heat. He paused beside a pile of peas
to get his breath back.

But then he noticed something very strange.

There was a small mountain of marrows opposite him. And there was something unusual about the marrow on top. Metal horns were sticking out from either end . . .

"Uh-oh," said Pat as he rose, ready to run. But then the marrows seemed to explode in all directions as T-117 the ter-moo-nator burst out of hiding! One of the big green

missiles slammed into Pat's stomach, and the other whapped into his head. Pat was knocked to the ground!

When he recovered, T-117 was standing over him, holding a ray gun.

"Subject confirmed as C.I.A. Agent Pat Vine," he droned.

"You set an ambush," Pat gasped. "How did you know I would come here?"

"I saw your Time Shed arrive," said T-117. "And I was hiding beneath the Circus when the fire went out. I heard Agent McMoo instruct you to return." The robo-bull smiled and its green eyes glowed brighter. "Agent McMoo helped us put out the fire. He will help us again."

"Oh yeah?" said Pat. "And what about me?"

The ter-moo-nator aimed its gun at Pat's nose. "You will help us too."

The last thing Pat saw was a beam of bright white light as T-117 opened fire . . .

Chapter Five

ROMAN KNOWS

Little Bo was lying on a bed of hay in a cattle pen, trying to get her strength back.

After winning her fight, she had been led here by the two gladiator bulls. A gladiator's outfit had been laid out for her on the hay, to go with her helmet. There was a breastplate, some kneepads and a skirt made of metal slats.

"Put on the shiny clothes," said one of the gladiators in a slow, halting voice.

"No way!" said Bo. "Bronze is so not my colour. I wouldn't be seen dead in an outfit like that!"

"Oh yeah?" said the other, with an

evil sneer. "Just you wait."

Bo picked up the breastplate. "I guess maybe I could make it work if I wore it with a pink crocodile-skin jacket and purple tights . . ."

"Put on the shiny clothes," the first bull repeated. "Or else."

Bo frowned. Why did cattle have to dress like human gladiators?

She puzzled over it as she finally got changed into the gladiator outfit. Then a loud gong sounded just outside her

pen, making her jump. A minute later, tough bulls started filing past, all in the same direction.

The last of the bulls went by. And then that weird, white water buffalo, Lanista, walked up to Bo's pen and opened the gate.

"You've rested long enough," he said. "It's time for stage two."

"Whatever," muttered Bo.

They walked through the maze of passageways until they reached a group of bull gladiators waiting outside a door. Lanista led them into a surprisingly modern classroom. There were thirty metal chairs and desks, and a large whiteboard at one end — technology from the future that the F.B.I. had brought back to the past.

"Now then, class," said Lanista, standing beside the whiteboard. "Today we welcome a new student — her name is Umm."

"What? Oh yeah." Bo had almost forgotten about her undercover name. "Yep, I'm Umm. Hi." She waved round the room and leaned back in her chair. The others just glared at her. One of them spat cud at her hooves, and Bo frowned. They looked a hard bunch.

"Now, this afternoon we are going to learn about directions," said Lanista with a sigh. "Yet again . . ." He took out a kind of remote control. "You – Brutus." The water buffalo pointed his huge horns at a mean-looking bull in the front row. "What is the opposite of down?"

Brutus shrugged. "Er . . . sideways?"

"NO!" snapped Lanista, and hit a button on the remote with his hoof. "It's 'up'!" With a loud BOING, Brutus went flying out of his seat and banged his head on the ceiling. He fell back down to the ground in a daze and snorted crossly.

"Hey!" Bo shouted. "What happened there?"

"Oh dear, did I forget to say?" Lanista chuckled nastily. "These chairs are not ordinary chairs. They are ejector seats! Whenever anyone gets a question wrong, they are sent flying into the ceiling."

Bo scowled. "That's mean!"

"Ooooh, that's meeeean," said one cow, doing an impression of Bo. The rest of the class laughed.

"Us not care about jumpy chairs," said Brutus, giving her an evil look. "Us TOUGH."

"My students must prove their strength in both the arena and the classroom," said Lanista grandly. "It is all part of the gladiator training. So, Umm . . . Which way is left?"

Bo sighed. "This is my left," she said. Then she pointed the other way. "And that's *your* left – which is my right."

Lanista smiled. "Very good."

"She teacher's pet!" rumbled a big bull at the back. He bashed his hooves together. "Us squash teacher's pets."

"That's enough, Julius," said Lanista. "Now then, Umm – what's the difference between forwards and backwards?"

"Duh!" Bo cried. "Forwards is when you walk forward, like this" – she jumped up, shoving her desk over as she did so – "and backwards is when you go into reverse – like this." She trotted back a few steps and whacked into her chair as hard as she could. With a loud SNAP it broke and landed with a clatter at Lanista's hooves.

To her amazement, Lanista started to laugh. "Excellent, young Umm. Not only do you have strength and fighting spirit, you have brains too." He looked at her, thoughtfully. "Yes, I think you can join the Elite."

"Elite?" Bo looked at him suspiciously. "What does that mean?"

"It means you have passed stage two," said Lanista. "I am going to put you into the Elite training class at the Circus Maximus at once!"

"Us get you, teacher's pet!" snarled Julius, and the whole class burst into angry mooing, sticking out their tongues and waggling their horns.

"Yeah," sneered Brutus. "There thirty of us and only one of you."

"Thirty to one?" Bo frowned. "Doesn't sound very fair."

"Us not fair," said Julius. "Us fight to win — as nasty as we can!"

Bo did her best to ignore the gladiators' guffaws as she followed the water buffalo from the room. "I don't like the sound of this Elite class," Bo muttered. "Oh, Pat, Professor — what have I gone and got myself into now?"

Chapter Six

THE EMPEROR'S MOO FRIEND

"Have more food, McMoo!" said Emperor Nero through a big mouthful of roast swan. He had been stuffing his face for two hours straight, throwing away bones and shells and spitting stuff out on to the marble dining-room floor for his servants to clear away. He lay down on a large cushion, surrounded by slave girls, and swigged deeply from a golden goblet. "And you must have some more wheat and honey wine!"

Professor McMoo wished longingly for a simple cup of tea. "No more for me, thanks!" he said as a slave girl took his plate away. While he wore his

ringblender, of course, she and Nero saw him as a Roman nobleman. If they knew he was really a bull, they would understand why he hadn't managed to eat much of the magnificent ten-course dinner. The stuffed dormouse and snails hadn't really appealed, and neither had the main dish – a whole pig, stuffed with sausages and fruit, roasted and served standing up.

"What's wrong, McMoo?" Nero

looked at him sternly. "Is my company not to your liking?"

"It's great," McMoo said quickly. "I just can't help worrying where my young friends have got to. Little Bo has been missing for ages – and Pat should have joined us here a long time ago."

"I am sure they will both turn up soon," said Nero. "But in the meantime . . . " He belched noisily. "You say you don't believe that the nasty fire beneath the Circus Maximus was started by a dodgy heating pipe. In which case – what *did* start it?"

McMoo leaned forward. "I'm afraid, great Nero, that the Roman Empire may have enemies hiding underground."

Nero stared. "Whatever do you mean?"

McMoo hesitated. He couldn't start talking about ter-moo-nators or bulls from the future – Nero would think he was a nutcase and throw him out. "I . . .

I think I saw someone down there. Someone who may be taking advantage of the Circus being closed to do something that is bad news for Rome – maybe even the whole world."

"Well, they'll have to be quick!" said Nero, tossing his empty goblet over his shoulder. "I'm opening the Circus again this very night."

"Oh yes," McMoo remembered. "A special event to cheer everyone up."

"That's right," said Nero. He glanced out of the window at a sundial. "Jumping Jupiter, is that the time? I must get to my private box in the Circus. I have to introduce the show. Why not come with me? You can look around afterwards. And if your young friends turn up here, my slaves will send them along to join you."

The professor bowed. "Thank you, great Nero!" Though he was still worried, McMoo perked up at the thought of a night at the Circus Maximus. What a piece of history that would be!

Professor McMoo rode through the streets of Rome with Nero in the emperor's personal chariot. It was only seven o'clock, and the skies were still blue and bright. Soon they were driving around the outside of the Circus Maximus to reach the private entrance. McMoo noticed Bessium Barmus in her

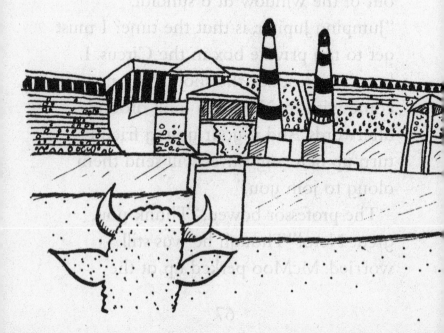

stall beneath the archway, selling tickets.

He sighed. Bessium's business seemed to be booming. He only hoped that with a ter-moo-nator on the loose, nothing else went "boom" tonight . . .

Once inside, McMoo found the Circus Maximus to be an incredible sight. The track was a massive, dusty oval, divided in the middle by a stone barrier that was hundreds of metres long. Stretching all around the track were rows upon rows of stands, filled with cheering,

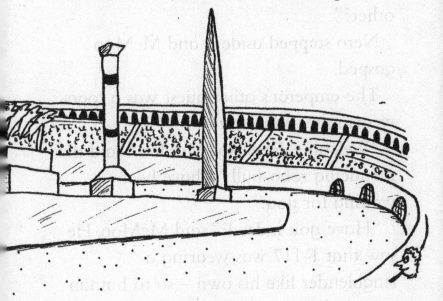

shouting Romans, excited at the thought of what sights the night might bring. The noise almost shook the professor's horns loose as he followed Nero and his guards up some stone steps. They led to the emperor's private box, a stone enclosure rising up from the stands directly opposite the finish line.

"Oh, I forgot to say!" Nero paused in the doorway to his private box and smiled at McMoo. "I've invited another guest. I wonder if you two know each other?"

Nero stepped aside – and McMoo gasped.

The emperor's other guest was a toga-wearing ter-moo-nator. T-117!

"Welcome, Professor McMoo," said the menacing robo-bull. "I have been waiting for you."

"Have you indeed?" said McMoo. He saw that T-117 was wearing a ringblender like his own – so to human eyes, he appeared human. Only cows could see through each other's disguises. "Who does Nero think you are?"

"I am Timon of Nator, a powerful nobleman from a far-off land," said the ter-moo-nator, smiling. "Is it not obvious?"

"Timon is my best friend," Nero declared. "I love him! Thanks to him, I am going to be Emperor of the World!"

"He's tricking you! Don't listen to him!" McMoo shouted. But the guards grabbed hold of him and forced him into the box. T-117's green eyes glowed more brightly as he watched the professor struggle.

"It's him, isn't it?" said Nero excitedly. "McMoo, the clever one you told me about. I did well, didn't I? Keeping him busy and then bringing him to you, I mean."

"Yes, Nero," said T-117. "You did well." Soon the professor found himself

helpless in a chair, with half-a-dozen
spears aimed at his head – and the
ter-moo-nator looming over him . . .

"Thank you, Professor, for putting out

the fire we started beneath the street," said T-117. "A little project of ours has developed a problem. It might have taken me weeks to put it right." He smiled. "But then I saw you had followed me to this time. And I knew that a genius like you would fix it double-quick."

"Well, you were wrong," snapped McMoo. "OK, apart from that bit about me being a genius — that was true." He scowled. "And since I *am* a genius, I bet I could fix your experiment in a few hours. But I won't!"

"Yes, you will," said Nero. "I command it! I am Emperor of Rome!"

"I don't care if you're Queen of Sheba, I will never help a ter-moo-nator!" McMoo glared at the robo-bull. "Whatever he's said, he doesn't want to help you, Nero. He wants to help the Fed-up Bull Institute take control of the world!"

But Nero had spied another sundial and wasn't listening. "Oooh, is that the time? I'd better introduce the evening's first attraction . . ."

The crowd roared with delight as their emperor waved to them from the box's balcony. "Hail, Nero!" they chanted, over and over again.

T-117 pressed his metal snout up against McMoo's ear. "You will help me," he hissed. "For if you do not . . . a terrible fate awaits your young friend Pat Vine."

McMoo nearly choked. "What?"

"I don't know where your girl assistant has got to," the ter-moo-nator admitted, "but I found the boy and brought him here earlier while you dined with Nero . . ."

"And now, ladies and gentlemen," Nero shouted to the crowd, "let's get the show rolling with some fabulous animal entertainment – lions against bulls!"

"Take a look, Professor," said the
ter-moo-nator mockingly. "And see if
you won't change your mind about
helping us."

Professor McMoo dived over to the
balcony. Down in the arena he saw
twelve huge, meaty lions prowling
towards four bulls – a skinny one, a tall
one and a short one . . .

And a young
bullock in a white
toga – Pat!

Chapter Seven

THE SECRET BENEATH

McMoo stared in horror as the lions roared and the crowds roared louder. "Nero, stop this at once!"

"Shan't!" said Nero. "They're only cattle, McMoo, what's your problem?"

The twelve angry lions stalked closer to the bulls, their huge jaws drooling . . .

"Help us, McMoo!" T-117 demanded. "Or else—"

"All right!" cried the professor helplessly. "Save the cattle and I'll do anything you ask!"

The ter-moo-nator nodded at Nero, who crossed to the balcony and raised both arms. Suddenly, a gateway opened

in the arena and four of Nero's guards rushed out to bundle the bulls to safety. The crowd booed and hissed. Then some proper gladiators came in to fight the lions, and they started cheering again.

"You are both horrible and cruel," said McMoo angrily. "What do you want me to do?"

"Come with me," said T-117, "and I shall show you . . ."

Pat couldn't believe his luck when the guards turned up from nowhere to whisk him away from the lions. If only they could have saved him from T-117 in the vegetable store. The robo-bull had blasted him with a stun ray, and when Pat woke up he found himself in a cold, stony cell in the heart of the Circus Maximus with his fellow prisoners. His ringblender had been taken away, but his gladiator helmet had a translator inside so he could still understand what people said. Or rather, what they shouted.

"Come on!" bellowed the guard leader. "If you don't get a move on you'll wish we had left you to the lions . . ."

Four guards had dragged them here – and now it seemed they were going to drag them back again. The guard leader pushed his prisoners forward at sword-point through the gloomy, torch-lit passageways.

But suddenly, a loud CLANG-CLANG-CLANG! echoed through the tunnel. Pat jumped and turned round – to find the three guards at the back slumping to the ground with crooked helmets and a dopey look on their faces.

The guard leader frowned. "Someone's whacked them!" he cried, staring all about. "Who's out there?"

Then a hoof flashed down from the

roof of the passageway and connected with the guard leader's head! As the human tottered and toppled over, Pat caught a glimpse of a bright blue udder hanging down from the ceiling.

"Little Bo!" he cried in delight.

"Shut up, big-mouth!" she hissed. "Or you'll bring more guards running!"

"Sorry," he said, reaching up to help her down. "How did you manage to stay up there?"

"Chewing gum!" Bo wiped her hooves and blew a pink bubble in his face.

Pat grinned and hugged her. "Most cows chew the cud – not gum!"

"Then it's a good job I'm not most cows," she said, hugging him back. "I'm so glad you're all right. I saw the guards take you down here from my classroom window, but I couldn't get out to save you until now."

"Classroom?" Pat frowned. "What are you on about?"

But Bo had turned to the other three bulls. "OK, boys, you had better get out of here. Follow this tunnel straight to the end and you'll reach the emergency exit. Don't stop running till you're right out of Rome."

"Thank you," mooed the skinny bull. "Sorry we had to fight you before." They saluted her and ran away.

Pat looked at his sister. "What's going on?"

"The F.B.I. is up to something big, Pat," Bo told him. "They are rounding up cattle and making them fight each other like gladiators. The toughest, brainiest fighters are taken to join the Elite – like me. The useless failures are taken here and thrown to the lions – like them!"

"I nearly went the same way." Pat shuddered. "But what's it all for? What *is* the Elite?"

"I'll tell you all I know," said Bo. "But first – where's the professor?"

"He's all right," said Pat. "He's made friends with Emperor Nero and gone to his palace."

"What?" Bo's eyes widened with horror. "Nero is the man behind this whole scheme, Pat. He's working with the ter-moo-nators!"

"Oh no!" Pat groaned. "We've got to warn the professor!"

But before they could move, they

heard the sound of hoofsteps coming from further up the tunnel.

"Quick," hissed Bo. "Let's get these sleeping guards out of sight and hide!"

They moved quickly, stuffing the guards in the storeroom and hiding behind the door as the sound got louder – lighter clips and clops mingling with the heavy stamp of metal hooves . . .

Pat had to stifle a gasp as T–117 the ter-moo-nator clanked past a storeroom door – with Professor McMoo firmly in his grip.

"We're too late," said Bo grimly. "The professor's a prisoner!"

Professor McMoo was led by the ter-moo-nator through a maze of dark, winding tunnels. Suddenly, ahead of him, came the same deep and powerful roar that he and Pat had heard while talking to Bessium Barmus. It was coming from behind a metal door in the wall.

"What is that noise?" McMoo demanded. "You know, above ground, they think it's a ghost."

"That is good," said T-117, shoving him towards the door. "Fear of ghosts keeps people away . . . so our secret underground workshop stays undiscovered."

"Workshop?" McMoo frowned. The roar behind the door was getting louder, building to a steady, throaty growl. The ter-moo-nator pressed a button and the door slid up – to reveal a vast chamber filled with red light.

It was as hot as an oven, and the noise was deafening. McMoo stuck his hooves in his ears. In the middle of the chamber stood something very long and very large, covered by a black protective sheet. But McMoo's attention was distracted by the goings-on in the rest of the room. Bulls in protective suits were smelting iron in one corner. Drums of oil were stacked in another. A sort of garage had been set up in the third corner, where bull mechanics were crowded around a large, metal framework. And in the fourth corner,

buffalo scientists were sitting at a long workbench, tinkering with hi-tech electronics and machine parts. The bone-shaking noise was coming from a huge, incredible engine, hanging on heavy wires from the ceiling.

"Switch it off!" bellowed T-117. A buffalo rushed to obey and the sound slowly died.

"So that's the so-called 'ghost's' roar," McMoo realized. "The roar of engines!"

"Correct," said the ter-moo-nator, crossing to the workbench with its electronic bits and bobs. "It was the engine that caused the fire. Each time we try to fit it with a mega-thrust power booster, it goes wrong."

"I recognize those parts," murmured McMoo. He turned to T-117. "They're the ones you stole from the Palace of Great Moos – bits from all the latest air-cars and travel-pods."

The ter-moo-nator smiled. "How else

can we make our engines the most powerful in history?"

McMoo looked at him worriedly. "But what are the engines for?"

T-117 strode over to the huge, dark shape in the middle of the chamber — and whipped away the covering sheet. McMoo stared in amazement. Beneath it stood a giant, chunky chariot made from gleaming metal. It had massive rubber wheels with metal spikes sticking out.

"The engines will power machines like this, Professor," cried the ter-moo-nator triumphantly. "The F.B.I. Roman war-wagon – the super-charged chariot that will change the face of history!"

Chapter Eight

THE RO-MOO-N EMPIRE

"So this is why you robbed so many electrical shops in your own time," McMoo realized. "To help you build this thing!"

"And to build all its weapons," said T-117, picking up a remote control. He pressed a button and a metal nozzle rose up from the chariot's roof. "This is a curdle cannon. It fires sour milk and runny cheese over a distance of half a mile – a mixture so smelly it leaves its victims helpless."

McMoo gasped as the nozzle fired a jet of stinky slush and splatted a target on the wall. The air filled with a deadly reek and he held his nose with both hooves. "What a pong!"

The ter-moo-nator picked up a large yellow gun. "And this is the butter bazooka. Anyone hit by its giant butter-bullets will become super-slippery. They won't be able to stand up without sliding about, and any weapons will slip from their grip . . ."

"But the people of ancient Rome aren't ready for advanced technology like this," McMoo protested. "If they have weapons like this in the first century, they won't live long enough to reach the second!"

"These chariots are designed to be used only by bulls," said T-117. "With Emperor Nero's unwitting support, the F.B.I. has been building a legion of Roman battle-cattle. Only the toughest, meanest gladiators get through – the rest are thrown to the lions."

McMoo scowled. "That's cold blooded moo-der!"

The ter-moo-nator just smiled. "Most of our gladiators will go into battle on their hoofs. But the brightest ones join the Elite – where they are trained to pilot the war-wagons." T-117's eyes glowed brighter. "Think of it, Professor. With such a powerful army, all Rome's enemies – from the forces of Egypt to the Barbarian hordes – will be buttered, battered and utterly defeated. The Roman Empire will grow and grow . . . and it will never fall!"

"But I don't understand," said McMoo. "Why are you fighting for Nero and his human empire?"

"We are not," hissed T-117. "Nero is a zero. He truly believes we want to make him Emperor of the World." The robo-bull laughed. "He has let us use the Circus Maximus and the cattle market to train gladiators and build our war-wagons. He has allowed us to build a fierce and fearsome F.B.I. army, right in the very heart of Rome."

T-117's smug voice rose higher and higher. "But before Nero can use the war-wagons against Rome's enemies . . . we shall use them against him!"

"Aha," said McMoo. "And once you've taken control of the largest empire in the world, you will conquer the rest of the planet."

"Precisely," snarled the ter-moo-nator. "Bulls will rule all! But first you must fix the fault with the engines so we can fit the mega-thrust power booster. With that, the war-wagons will be able to soar over any obstacles in their way. Nothing will stop them!"

"Ah, yes, well . . ." said McMoo shiftily, eyeing the buffalo scientists and their electronic bric-a-brac. "This is clearly a very clever bit of kit. It could take me weeks to understand it, months even . . ."

"Do not play for time, Professor," T-117 warned him. "You will work with our buffalo scientists. I want the power-boosters ready for testing within twenty-four hours." The ter-moo-nator's eyes glowed bright and green. "Otherwise, your puny friend Pat will be thrown to the lions once more – and you with him!"

"That wicked, evil ter-moo-nator,"
muttered Pat. At that very moment, he
and Bo were hiding just outside the
workshop doorway, straining to catch
every word that was being said. "And
the poor professor. If only I could let
him know I'm safe!"

"If you did, you wouldn't stay that
way for long." Bo sighed. "I knew those
war-wagons spelled trouble. I've been
test-driving them with the Elite around
the Circus all afternoon. Once the
professor adds a power booster to the
engines, they'll be unstoppable."

"And the F.B.I. will take over the
world," said Pat miserably. "They will
turn all cows into crazy warlike
creatures . . . and the future will turn
into dung. Oh, if only we could rescue
the professor!"

"I doubt if even he can do much
against that army of gladiators down at

the cattle market," said Bo sadly. "They're a tough, mean bunch."

"Hang on!" said Pat, peering past her down the passageway. "I think someone's coming – hide!" He dragged Bo into a small alcove in the tunnel wall – and just in time. Moments later, Lanista the white water buffalo came marching up to the workshop in a purple-edged toga. His horns were so pointy and wide he had to turn sideways just to get through the doorway.

"Ter-moo-nator T-117, report!" he shouted.

Leaving McMoo hard at work with the scientists, T-117 clanked over. "Yes, Agent Lanista?"

"We must speed up our plans," said the water buffalo. "Now we know the C.I.A. has broken through our time shields and sent agents here, we can't delay. Soon they may arrive in force. We must take over Rome as soon as possible." He looked over at McMoo. "Do you think the professor can solve the mega-thrust problem?"

"Yes," said the ter-moo-nator. "He will not let his friend come to harm. There is a ninety-nine per cent probability that the power booster will be working by tomorrow afternoon."

"Then we should test it in action," said Lanista. "Tell Nero to open the Circus Maximus for a special chariot race tomorrow night at eight o'clock. I shall make sure that everyone vital to the running of Rome comes to watch –

and that they are sitting in a special location." He smiled. "These worthy Romans will make fine targets for the war-wagons' curdle cannons and butter bazookas – and then we shall give the emperor himself a good sloshing!"

Bo and Pat had to put a hoof over each other's mouths to stifle their gasps.

"Excellent, Agent Lanista," said T-117 with a mechanical laugh. "With Rome's wisest leaders out of the way, its people will have no one to turn to. Our army of cruel gladiators will catch them and make them into slaves."

Lanista nodded. "Slaves who will build us more and more war-wagons with

working mega-thrust power boosters –
craft with the ability to leap buildings
and travel over any terrain . . ." He
threw back his head and laughed. "The
Roman Empire will soon become the
Ro-MOO-n Empire!" he cried. "This
will be a chariot race no one will ever
forget!"

Chapter Nine

THE BEST LAID PLANS OF MOOS AND MEN

Pat and Bo held their breath as T-117 went back to guard Professor McMoo in the workshop, and as Lanista strode away back down the passage.

"Should I nip after old handlebar-horns and punch his lights out?" wondered Bo.

"That won't change what they're planning, will it?" Pat sighed. "The F.B.I. will still have their chariots and their evil army over at the cattle market."

"Well, what *do* we do, smarty-pants?" Bo glared at him. "I'm the one who's going to have to drive one of those

dumb war-wagons tomorrow."

"Actually, that gives me an idea," said Pat. "I'd better get out of here and after Lanista."

"How are you going to do that?" Bo folded her arms. "You've lost your ringblender, remember? Any guard who spots a wandering bullock will raise the alarm!"

"Aha," said Pat, reaching into his toga pocket. "But I still have the ringblender I was going to give to you before T-117 cow-napped me!" He snapped it in place and sighed. "Of course, I'm not sure the pink polka dots are really my style, but it will do."

"And what about me?" Bo complained.

"Whatever happens, Bo, you must stay undercover," Pat told her. "Don't be mouthy, don't try to rescue the professor, and definitely don't punch anyone."

She grinned. "You're asking a lot, Pat."

"We're going to need you behind the wheel of a war-wagon tomorrow," said Pat. "OK?"

"All right, little bruv," said Bo. "But whatever your idea is, I hope it works. Or else, all history . . . is history!"

Pat followed Lanista through the gloomy stone passages, as the water buffalo took a secret exit out of the Circus Maximus. He had slipped Bo's ringblender through his nose, so to human eyes he would look like a young boy and not a desperate cow agent on the run. As it was, he managed to make it out into the warm evening without being spotted.

Lanista walked around the outside of the Circus until he saw Bessium Barmus. She was sitting beneath her arch counting coins and looking very sorry for herself. He marched up to her, and Pat listened in on their conversation from behind a pillar.

"Hey, ticket woman," said the water buffalo. He was wearing a ringblender too, and in his purple-edged toga Bessium saw him as a fine nobleman. "I have been sent by Emperor Nero to bring you good news."

"Oh yeah?" said Bessium grumpily. "Like what?"

"Tomorrow night, at eight o'clock, the emperor is holding the first of his all-new, super-snazzy, extra-whizzy chariot races. It'll be the most talked about event of the century!"

"YESSSS!" Bessium jumped up in delight, her flab wobbling. "I can charge special prices! Three people get in for the price of five . . ." She was starting to dribble. "I'll make a mint!"

"But," Lanista added, "it's vitally important you let some special people in entirely free."

Bessium stopped dribbling. In fact, she looked like she'd just swallowed a maggot the size of a sock. "F-f-free?"

"Free," Lanista insisted, and handed her a scroll. "Hurry around the city tonight and give a free ticket to everyone on this list. Make sure they arrive nice and early – and make very sure they are all sitting together on the seats beneath the emperor's private box."

"Why should I?" Bessium spat.

"Because if you don't, Nero will throw you to the lions," snarled Lanista, "and we'll see how many tickets you'll sell for *that*!" But then he smiled charmingly. "And because if you do, I will give you a hundred gold coins!"

"Gold coins? Gold?" Bessium looked like all her Christmases had come at once, along with several birthdays and one or two Easters. "It's a deal!"

Hidden behind his pillar, Pat nodded grimly. "So that's how the F.B.I. will get the leaders of Rome together for target practice," he muttered. "By relying on Bessium's greed for cash!"

Bessium had started doing a very strange version of the conga in and out of her archway. She reached out her arms for Lanista, who turned his back and started to walk away. "Just make sure you don't mess up, woman," he warned her. "You must get everybody on that list to that very spot in the Circus – or else you'll be giving those lions indigestion for weeks!"

But Bessium hardly heard him. She was too busy dancing and jiggling all about. "I'm rich!" she yelled, closing her eyes and throwing Lanista's scroll up in the air . . .

It fell right into Pat's hooves!

"Eh?" Bessium opened her eyes again and looked all about her. "Where did that stupid scroll go?"

Frantically, Pat unrolled the scroll behind his pillar. He had a plan, but he knew he didn't have long. Dipping a hoof in some soot on the ground from the fire that afternoon, he scrawled something at the bottom of Lanista's list. Then he rolled it back up and tossed it over his shoulder.

"Aha – that's where the stupid thing landed," said Bessium, grabbing it and plodding away. "Suppose I'd better get going . . ."

"And so had I," murmured Pat to himself, hurrying back down the street and turning right towards the Circus. "I must try to get a message to the professor, to tell him I'm OK . . ."

"But you're *not* OK, are you, Pat Vine?" said a voice behind him.

"In fact, you're in big trouble!"

Pat whirled round to find Lanista had stepped out of hiding. His heart sank as he saw the water buffalo was pointing a small gun straight at him.

"I don't know how you got away from the Circus," Lanista went on, "but you won't walk free again. I'm going to keep a watch on you myself – all night long. This time there will be no escape!"

Chapter Ten

RAISING THE ROOF
(WITH A HOOF AND AN OOF)

In the F.B.I.'s secret workshop, Professor McMoo wiped the sweat from his forehead. The buffalo scientists lay

asleep all around him. He had been working on the mega-thrust power boosters all night, all morning and most of the afternoon — without a single cup of tea!

But he'd been so worried about Pat and Bo he had hardly noticed. Pat was a prisoner, of course — but what on earth had happened to the boy's sister?

The door slid open and T-117 came clanking in. "It is almost six o'clock," he bellowed, jerking the scientists awake. "Have you fixed the power boosters yet, Professor?"

"Just about," McMoo admitted, picking up the rocket-shaped booster. "It's a simple case of reversing the oil-flux power-feed and changing the polarity of the ignition vectors. I don't know why you didn't think of it yourself!"

"Finish the work," the ter-moo-nator commanded.

"No!" McMoo dropped the booster onto the workbench. "Not until I know that Pat is safe and well!"

"Funny you should say that . . ." Lanista the water buffalo walked in —

holding Pat in a hooflock.

"Pat!" McMoo beamed.

"I'm sorry, Professor." Pat sighed. "I got away, but they caught me again and locked me up."

"I'm glad to see you," McMoo told him. "Are you all right?"

Lanista scowled. "He won't be for long unless the power boosters work!"

"Yes, well," said McMoo. "I've just got a few more minor modifications to make."

"Your time has run out," hissed T-117.

"Fine," said McMoo. "I'll stop. Throw Pat and me to the lions, if you like. But if you do, you'll never find out how I was going to boost the power in your power boosters by fifty per cent ..."

T-117's eyes grew as wide as saucers. "Fifty per cent?"

"That would give the war-wagons the power to jump a small mountain!" cried Lanista. "All right. We've still got two

hours before the show kicks off . . . Get on with it!"

"Yes, sir," said McMoo with a tiny smile to himself. He had just had an idea . . .

Up above, in the arena of the Circus Maximus, Bo was practising driving her war-wagon around the track. The controls were quite simple, so that cattle could work them. You pulled or pushed on a big joystick to steer yourself about. One hoof worked the speed pedal, and one worked the brake. You worked the butter bazooka with your nose and the curdle cannon with your spare hooves.

She looked out of the plastic window and saw other gladiators trying to steer their own wagons. They were getting better and better at it. And they seemed to be getting better at firing the guns too. For now, all they were firing was water. But Bo knew that would soon change . . .

"Maybe I could attack the other war-wagons?" she murmured to herself. "Stop them before they open fire?" But no, there were twelve of the mega-chariots trundling around the track. She wouldn't be able to stop them all . . .

"All right, playtime's over!" Emperor Nero's voice came crackling over her war-wagon's communicator. "Go back to the garages. The audience are ready to take their seats, and I want your chariots to come as a surprise . . ."

Bo stuck her chariot into reverse and sighed. "They'll be a surprise all right," she said.

"Time's up, McMoo," snarled Lanista, tightening his grip on Pat's hoof. "There's just an hour to go before the show starts. Everyone's taking their seats. I want that booster now."

"All right, all right, don't get your toga in a twist," said McMoo. "I've finished!" He picked up the booster and crossed to the large engine hanging from its wires in the middle of the chamber. He clipped it onto the side, then pressed a button on a remote control. The engine throbbed and roared into noisy life.

"Right then," shouted McMoo over the din. "We'll just let it warm up a bit . . ."

"Activate the booster," said T–117 impatiently.

"Yes," snapped Lanista. "I want to fit it to a war-wagon before the show starts – if it works, that is."

"If it works?" McMoo looked shocked. "What a cheek! I've made it five times more powerful than your silly scientists ever could. Take a look at this!"

He jabbed his hoof against the remote and switched on the booster. With a colossal bang, a huge jet of fire zoomed out — sending the entire engine flying up in the air! It snapped through its supporting wires and smashed into the stone roof of the workshop, as if trying to burrow its way out into the Circus above. Scientists and smelters squealed in a panic. T-117 and Lanista staggered back as rubble rained down and the whole room shook.

"Time for action, Pat!" shouted McMoo. He grabbed one of the wires now dangling from the crumbling ceiling, swung on it like a rope — and smashed right into the ter-moo-nator, sending him flying!

At the same time, Pat twisted free of Lanista's grip and butted him in the belly. The water buffalo snarled in fury and was about to charge – when a lump of falling stone conked him on the head. He fell to the floor in a daze.

"Good work!" McMoo shouted, switching off the engine before the whole roof came down. "Now, run!"

The two of them charged out of the workshop.

"Come back!" hollered T-117.

"Not likely!" McMoo shouted as they ran off down the gloomy tunnel.

"Well done, Professor!" cried Pat. "You tricked them!"

"Only partly," said McMoo. "The booster works properly now, and it really is fifty per cent more powerful."

A heavy clanking noise started up behind them. The ter-moo-nator was running after them! McMoo and Pat forced themselves to run even faster.

"Our only chance is to destroy those war-wagons before they enter the arena," McMoo panted. "If the F.B.I. fit them all with power boosters, they will never be stopped!"

The professor and Pat ran as fast as they could. They followed the sound of roaring engines all the way to the Circus garages. Gleaming war-wagons were lined up in front of a huge gateway, their engines growling, ready and waiting to enter the arena.

"Everybody out!" McMoo yelled. Not stopping for breath, he lowered his horns and charged at the nearest war-wagon's spiky rubber wheel, bursting it with a noisy hiss of air. "Showtime is over."

"Right!" shouted Pat, forcing open the door of the wagon with his horns and dragging out the surprised cow driver. "These wagons must never leave this garage!"

"Oh, but they will!" came a grinding,

mechanical growl from behind them.
T-117 had caught them up! He aimed
his death ray and opened fire . . .

Chapter Eleven

ASSAULT AND BUTTERY

McMoo and Pat dived for cover from the burning heat. "Hide behind a war-wagon, Pat!" McMoo shouted. "He won't dare open fire and risk damaging one of them."

"OK, Professor," said Pat, pointing behind them. "But what about those guards? Their swords and daggers won't hurt the war-wagons, but they'll turn us into pin-cushions!"

McMoo whirled round to find a dozen armed Romans were running towards them! "We're trapped," he cried. "If the guards don't get us, the ter-moo-nator will!"

Then, suddenly, with a roar of engines and a screech of whizzing tyres, one of the war-wagons came zooming towards them in reverse.

"And now we're going to get squished!" Pat groaned, closing his eyes . . .

But the chariot rushed past them – and crashed into T-117! With a loud bump and an electronic moo, he went flying into the garage wall.

"Jump on board!" yelled the cow at the wheel of the war-wagon, sticking her head out of the window.

It was Little Bo!

"Nice work, Bo!" cried McMoo, charging over to the chariot and jumping on board to give her a hug. "I've been so worried about you!"

"I'm still worried about her," said Pat as he wriggled into the driver's cabin beside Bo and the professor. "And us too for that matter!"

"All Elite Officers," screamed T-117. "Get the cow traitors in that war-wagon! Stop them! Squish them! Smash them!"

"I see what you mean," yelled Bo, stamping on the accelerator. "Time to get out of here!"

The war-wagon sped towards the huge garage gates – and knocked them down with a splintering crash. Then the chariot's chunky tyres kicked up huge clouds of dust as it shot off around the track. The audience were still taking their seats, and they had never seen anything like a war-wagon before. Some cheered, many screamed, and several hundred fainted on the spot.

"Stop it!" shouted Nero, waving his fist at Bo. "You've ruined my big build-up! My amazing intro! I was up all night rehearsing it!"

Bo blew a raspberry at him. "Professor," she said, "we've got to stop the F.B.I. from splatting Nero and the rulers of Rome with the war-wagons' weapons – before we're splatted ourselves!"

"Pat told me his plan as we hoofed it down here," said McMoo. "I only hope it works . . ."

But even as he spoke, the other working war-wagons came roaring out into the arena. Their huge spiky wheels tore up the track, their armoured shells shunted against each other as their drivers rushed to obey T-117's orders – to stop, squish and smash the runaway war-wagon.

"If they want a chase, I'll give them one!" shouted Bo. McMoo and Pat gasped in alarm as she jiggled the joystick this way and that, throwing them from side to side as they skidded all over the track. Their war-wagon's tyres threw up a dust storm, and the crowd's cheering turned to choking. The

thick yellow cloud blinded the drivers of the wagons right behind them. They smashed into each other, then crashed against the long strip of stone in the centre of the arena.

"Wa-heyyy!" yelled Bo. "Three down, seven to go!"

"Change of orders!" T-117's voice rattled out over every war-wagon's speakers. "Abandon chase. Set butter bazookas to full blast and curdle cannons to critical. Open fire on sector alpha-one. Repeat, sector alpha-one!"

"Oh no," cried McMoo. "Where's that?"

"Nero's private box and the seats underneath it," Bo told him. "And with seven war-wagons, the F.B.I. can't miss!"

"I hope they can't, anyway," said Pat.

"What?" Bo frowned. "What do you mean?"

McMoo was smiling. "Because Pat's

plan depends on these wagons scoring a direct hit!"

"You've both gone crazy!" Bo complained. "In case you'd forgotten, the F.B.I. is going to butter-blitz and curdle Rome's most important people!"

Pat laughed and pointed through the dust clouds. "Not if something else gets in their way!"

Bo stared in amazement as the war-wagon burst through the dust . . . to reveal that the seats below the emperor's box were crammed full of hundreds and hundreds of tough, mean bull gladiators!

"But I don't get it," said Bo. "What are *they* doing there?"

"Lanista gave Bessium a list of all the V.I.P.s he wanted her to bring along," Pat explained. "I just added a line at the end – *But only if there's room once you've brought all the nasty dressed-up bulls from the cattle market!*"

"And with all this dust blocking his view, old robo-chops the ter-*poo*-nator hasn't noticed!" Bo laughed. "They'll be zapping their own army! And I might as well be the first to . . . open fire!"

Bo waggled her horns and the war-wagon's butter bazooka burst into life. Gallons of slippery sludge gushed from the gun. With a nudge of her udder she set the curdle cannons going too.

Super-sour and stinky dairy destruction rained down on the gladiator bulls. They coughed and spluttered and slid about all over the place.

"Us not care!" mooed Brutus. "Us stink anyway!"

Some of the crowd thought the attack was part of the show, and started to laugh and cheer.

"Direct hit!" shouted Bo, driving away as the other war-wagons joined in the attack.

"Change of orders again!" squawked the ter-moo-nator's voice over the speakers as he realized his mistake. But before he could say another word, Professor McMoo punched a hole in the communicator and touched two wires together. A high-pitched whistle came out of the speakers.

"Ha!" said McMoo with satisfaction. "I've just transmitted a negative wave that should jam T-117's signals. Now he can't tell his drivers what to do."

"So they'll keep on firing!" Bo realized, parking her war-wagon a safe distance away so they could watch the action. "Those gladiators were trained to fight – let's see how they do!"

The butter bombardment and clots of curdled cream kept raining down on the gladiators. Bessium Barmus was skidding around in front of them, coated in the stuff. The smell was suffocating.

"Pack it in!" Bessium yelled uselessly at the war-wagons. "You're spoiling it for the emperor's Very Important Guests! Go and attack the cheap seats over there!"

"Yes, stop it, you rotten lot!" screamed Nero, hopping up and down with rage on the balcony of his box. "My big show is ruined!" But then he was hit in the chest by a cream-cheese blast, and with a horrified shout, he fell! "Arrrgh. . ."

"Look!" gasped Pat.

"What a horrible sight!" cried Bo.

BOING! Bessium's billowing belly had broken Nero's fall! They both flopped to the sticky ground.

T-117 came clanking up. He raised his ray gun, but a butter-burst knocked it flying. "Ticket woman, you have brought the wrong people," he groaned, clutching his metal head as he was sprayed and splattered. "You were meant to bring the wisest people in all of Rome!"

"Only if there was room, metal-mush!" Bessium weakly showed him her soggy scroll. "See?"

By now, some of the gladiators were fighting back. "Us can take on anything!" roared Brutus.

"Me LIKE the taste of rotten butter," his friend revealed, and many of the other gladiators seemed to agree with him.

"Stampede! Stampede!" shouted Brutus. The battle-cattle slipped and splashed but kept smashing up the war-wagons. They slashed the tyres with their spears and swords. They broke the windows with their bare, buttery hooves.

"Everything has gone wrong!" cried T-117, pitching forward into a putrid puddle of milky butter. "We have been tricked!"

"Yep!" called Professor McMoo as he, Pat and Bo burst out of their war-wagon. "You certainly have!"

"But you shall not enjoy the victory, McMoo," sneered the ter-moo-nator.

He pointed with a slippery, smelly hoof back towards the garage. Suddenly, a war-wagon jumped out from inside like a massive metal monster. The watching crowds gasped with amazement. One of the wagon's wheels was punctured, but that hardly seemed to matter. Blasts of flame shot from its base as it jumped through the air once more — heading towards the professor and his friends. And a furious face crowned with enormous horns was glaring out at them through the window.

"Lanista!" said Bo grimly.

McMoo nodded. "He's fitted that war-wagon with my mega-thrust power booster!"

"Then he's faster than us," Pat realized. "And that thing can chase us anywhere. There's nowhere to hide!"

Chapter Twelve

CHARIOTS OF FIRE

"Don't give up yet, Pat," said McMoo, pulling a remote control from his toga.

Bo frowned. "This is no time to be watching TV, Professor!"

But Pat recognized the gadget at once. "That's the control you used when you set off the power booster!"

"Correct!" said McMoo, pointing it at Lanista's war-wagon as it leaped towards them. "And once it gets into range . . ."

The professor hit a big red button.

Nothing happened.

Lanista's war-wagon jumped again, flying through the air and crashing

132

down on top of the other war-wagons, sending gladiator cows slipping and scattering. He was almost on top of Pat, Bo and McMoo.

"Um, Professor?" said Bo, blowing a gum bubble. "When exactly will it get into range?"

"Good question," said McMoo. With a cackle of triumph, Lanista hit the boosters once more and rose up in the air to crush them . . . "And here's a good answer!"

The professor hit the button again, and the boosters blasted into fiery life.

They blazed at least ten times more brightly, sending the war-wagon spiralling out of control, high up in the air above the arena.

McMoo winked at his friends. "You didn't think I'd actually give the F.B.I. a super-improved mega-thrust power booster without fitting a self-destruct switch, did you?"

The war-wagon tumbled helplessly like litter in the wind as the thruster jets slowly burned themselves out. The crowds yelled with fear, fleeing the arena.

"Whoooooooaaaaa!" yelled Lanista as he was sent somersaulting out through the window . . .

"He's gonna go splat!" Bo cried.

But in fact, Lanista landed in the sticky, slippery arms of the ter-moo-nator – and they both collapsed into the smelliest, most disgusting puddle of gunk in the whole arena. Moments later, the

F.B.I. agents were trampled by their own army, running away in panic.

"Oi! Posh-chops!" bellowed Bessium Barmus as Lanista splashed about in the buttery soup. "What about that bag of gold you promised me? I want it now!"

"Mission abort . . ." croaked T-117, skidding about as he tried to stand on his silver-platter time machine. "Retreat! Mission abort . . ."

"Wait for me!" gurgled Lanista, splashing and sliding in the slime until he grabbed hold of the ter-moo-nator's leg. Then they both disappeared in a haze of black smoke.

"Nooooooo!" wailed Bessium.

"We beat them!" Pat cheered. "We won!"

Bo pointed up at the war-wagon wheeling through the late evening sky. "But what goes up, must come down . . ."

As McMoo, Pat and Bo watched, the

thruster jets spluttered and stopped. The war-wagon dropped from the sky like a stone. It smashed into the middle of the arena and exploded in an enormous fireball – which soon set fire to the empty wooden seats at the back of the arena.

"Uh-oh," said Pat as the flames started to spread. "This is bad news."

"It's not just news," McMoo told him. "It's history," he beamed down at his two friends. "Pat, Bo – I think we just

started the Great Fire of Rome!"

Bo shot him a look. "Typical!"

"You said the fire started near the Circus," Pat recalled.

"And look over there," said McMoo, smiling.

Nero had dragged himself inside one of the broken war-wagons and was wrestling with the dead controls. "Work, curse you!" he shouted. "You're meant to be making me Emperor of the World!"

"Emperor of the Losers, more like," said Bessium, with a face more sour than the muck she was splashing in. "Stop fiddling about with that thing and get out of here!"

"So the historians were right," said McMoo. "Nero *did* fiddle while Rome burned!"

The fire spread to another abandoned war-wagon, which blew up before their eyes. "Come on," said Bo, eyeing the remaining crowds as they scattered in fright. "Everyone else is running for it. Let's make like bananas – and split!"

McMoo, Pat and Bo hurried away through the streets of Rome towards the Time Shed. A huge cloud of black smoke hung over the arena.

"The fire will do untold damage to Rome," said McMoo sadly. "But at least it will also wipe away all trace of the F.B.I.'s evil plot. Their underground agents will be long gone by now."

"What happens to Nasty Nero?" asked Pat.

"He builds an enormous golden palace for himself in the middle of the burned-down bit," said McMoo. "That doesn't make him very popular. He comes to a rather sticky end, I'm afraid."

"Stickier than all that curdled milk and cheese and butter?" Bo grinned. "I don't believe it!"

They got inside the Time Shed, and the professor quickly set the controls. "Right," he said. "Better get back to our own time and tell Yak the good news . . ."

"Yak has heard the good news, team!" came a gruff, familiar voice from the Time Shed's computer screen. "And he's smelled it too, let me tell you."

"Yak!" Bo cheered. "How's it going?"

"Good, thanks to you!" The black bull smiled and stepped aside to reveal T-117 and Lanista lying in a heap on a marble floor. "These stinky guys just turned up from nowhere, weak as kittens."

"We spoiled all their plans!" said Bo proudly.

Pat was puzzled. "But how did they end up with Yak?"

"In all the confusion, T-117 must have reversed the settings on his time machine to get away," McMoo explained. "It took him straight back to the time and place he'd visited last."

"Which was the Palace of Great Moos in 2550!" Bo grinned. "They landed right in Yak's lap!"

"And now they'll go to Bull Prison for a long time," said Yak. "Well done, team. You did the C.I.A. proud today. And here's your reward . . ."

In a flash of light, a large box appeared on the Time Shed's floor.

"Tea bags!" cried McMoo in delight. "A new supply of delicious twenty-sixth century tea!"

Yak waved and winked, and the screen went dark.

McMoo started kissing the tea bags. "Let's brew them up at once," he suggested. "I'm parched!"

"But, Professor," said Pat anxiously, "you made us leave the farm in such a hurry that Bo broke a fence. Back in our own time, Bessie Barmer's on the rampage."

"That's true," Bo remembered. "She was about to barge in here when you took off."

"Oh no!" moaned McMoo. "She'll want to threaten us and shout at us . . . I won't get my tea for ages!"

"Chill, Professor," Bo told him. She blew another gum bubble in his face. "A good plan is always worth reusing . . ."

The Time Shed landed back on the farm just a split-second after it had left. Bessie blinked and so missed the little glitch in reality – she never noticed a thing. She lumbered up to the wooden doors, braced herself, and then threw them open . . .

"Right, you beefy beggars," she snarled. "I'm gonna—"

Suddenly she stopped, and frowned, and stared all around. The shed was empty.

"Bah," she said. "I could have sworn they came in here." She bunched up her fists. "Well, I'll just have to search every inch of this farm! I'll get them in the end – especially the girl! Oooh, I'd like to be like my famous ancestor Bessium. I'd cook her up Roman-style – then I'd really be *glad-I-ate'er* . . .".

Chuckling at her nasty little joke, she thumped away with her stomach growling. And so she didn't notice that right above her head, McMoo, Pat and Bo were stuck to the rafters – thanks to blobs of Bo's bubble gum on their hooves!

Bo chuckled. "She'll be searching for us a long time!"

"More than long enough for us to put the kettle on," McMoo agreed happily, unpeeling his hooves from the roof. "We deserve a cuppa after solving that Roman moo-stery."

Pat and Bo dropped down to join him.

"I hope we get sent on another mission soon," said Pat.

"We will, little bruv, you'll see," Bo told him. "Yak will be getting on to us again in no time."

"No time? Nonsense!" McMoo grinned at her as he dropped tea bags in three cups. "Time is something we'll never run out of. We'll go on roaming through history for the C.I.A. for ever and ever — just you wait and see!"

THE END

C.I.A COWS IN ACTION

IT'S 'UDDER' MADNESS!

Genius cow Professor McMoo and his trusty sidekicks, Pat and Bo, are star agents of the C.I.A. – short for COWS IN ACTION! They travel through time, fighting evil bulls from the future and keeping history on the right track . . .

When Professor McMoo invents a brilliant TIME MACHINE, he and his friends are soon attacked by a terrifying TER-MOO-NATOR — a deadly robo-cow who wants to mess with the past and change the future! And that's only the start of an incredible ADVENTURE that takes McMoo, Pat and Bo from a cow paradise in the future to the SCARY dungeons of King Henry VIII . . .

It's time for action.

COW-ER WITH FEAR!

Genius cow Professor McMoo and his trusty sidekicks, Pat and Bo, are star agents of the C.I.A. – short for COWS IN ACTION! They travel through time, fighting evil bulls from the future and keeping history on the right track...

In ANCIENT EGYPT, a monstrous *moo-my* has come to life and kicked the PHARAOH off his throne. Sent to investigate, the C.I.A. agents face PERIL in the pyramids and nightmares on the Nile. Can they foil a TERRIFYING time-crime before the whole WORLD falls to the moo-my's curse?

It's time for action.

Collect them all!